D0606432

GRAPHIC TALES OF THE SUPERNATURAL

VAMPIRES

LEGENDS OF THE UNDEAD

written and illustrated by

Rob Shone

New York

Published in 2011 by The Rosen Publishing Group, Inc.
29 East 21st Street, New York, NY 10010

Designed and produced by
David West Books

Photo credits:
4t, Rama; 5t, Sfu; 5mr, Donovan Govan; 5ml, shutter.chick; 7m, Work Projects Administration Federal Art Project; California; 44, Nyki m.

Library of Congress Cataloging-in-Publication Data

Shone, Rob.
 Vampires : legends of the undead / Rob Shone. -- 1st ed.
    p. cm. -- (Graphic tales of the supernatural)
 Includes bibliographical references and index.
 ISBN 978-1-4488-1903-4 (library binding) -- ISBN 978-1-4488-1908-9
(pbk.) -- ISBN 978-1-4488-1915-7 (6-pack)
 1. Vampires--Comic books, strips, etc. I. Title.
 BF1556.S56 2010
 398.21--dc22

                                                2010025860

Manufactured in China

CPSIA Compliance Information Batch #DW1102YA:
For further information contact Rosen Publishing, New York, New York, at 1-800-237-9932.

CONTENTS

VAMPIRES: A SUPERNATURAL HISTORY

The vampire has a very long history. A fragment of 11,000-year-old Persian pottery shows a man fighting a blood-sucking monster. Nearly every culture from every country has stories of blood-drinking spirits that torment and terrorize.

A 3,000-year-old Assyrian bronze plaque designed to ward off the vampire god, Lamashtu.

LAND OF THE VAMPIRE

Most of the vampire myths and stories that we know today originated in the Balkan region of southeast Europe— Serbia, Albania, Romania, Bulgaria, and Greece. In Serbia, they were called *vampir*, and, in Greece, they were *vrykolakas*. The Albanian *lugat* was considered quite harmless, and a Bulgarian *ubour* would only drink blood as a last resort. Another kind of vampire was the *strigoi* from Romania. These were close relatives of werewolves. They were especially dangerous because they could change into a variety of animals. Vampires were found north of the Balkans. In Russia, they were called *upyr* and attacked children. In Poland, the *wapierz* slept in blood, while the Ukranian *upir* was thought to be fond of fish.

THE VAMPIRE HOMELAND

RUSSIA
Upyr

POLAND
Wapierz

UKRAINE
Upir

SERBIA
Vampir

CROATIA
Vampir

ROMANIA
Strigoi

BULGARIA
Ubour

KOSOVO
Vampir

ALBANIA
Lugat

GREECE
Vrykolakas

A Spotter's Guide to Vampires

There are many ways of returning from the dead as a vampire. Being bitten by one is the most well known. A cat or dog jumping over a corpse, rebelling against the church, being a witch, or simply being wicked—these are all ways to become one of the undead. Today, vampires are depicted as being pale and thin. However, the original Balkan vampire was described as red-faced and bloated with blood. Blood might be seen around the mouth, nose, and shroud, and the hair, nails, and teeth could all appear to have grown. And watch out for people who do not cast a shadow, have no reflection, or are afraid of sunlight. These are all vampire signs!

Coffins and crypts (above) are the homes and haunts of vampires. Garlic (left) is the healthy option–when it comes to keeping you vampire-free!

Vampire Proofing

Garlic, holy water, poppy seeds, and hawthorn branches are all charms used to keep vampires at bay. The vampire hunters' preferred method of killing a vampire was a wooden stake driven through its heart. Cutting off its head and burning the body could also work. In some Balkan countries, vampires could be shot or drowned, and a corpse might be pinned to the ground to stop it from rising.

Anti-vampire kits like this one (above) were useful for travelers to the Balkans in the 19th century. The engraving (right) shows 18th-century vampire hunters.

DRACULA: THE ULTIMATE VAMPIRE

The most famous vampire of them all is Count Dracula. The novel *Dracula* was written in 1897 by Irish author Bram Stoker and has remained popular ever since.

COUNT DRACULA: A GOTHIC HORROR

The novel tells of the vampire Count's attempt to take over the world and how he is defeated. Stoker spent nearly ten years carefully researching vampires and vampire lore for the book. Stoker's Count is nowadays seen as the classic vampire, but he is actually a mixture of different vampire habits and characteristics.

Vlad Dracula (above) (1431–1476) was also known as Vlad Tepes and Vlad the Impaler. He executed his enemies by impaling them on spikes.

Bram Stoker (left) (1847–1912) wrote other novels as well as Dracula.

VLAD DRACULA: SON OF THE DRAGON

Stoker's vampire was originally going to be called "Count Vampyr." Then, in his research Stoker discovered Vlad Dracula, Prince of Wallachia. When Dracula came to power, Wallachia was lawless and threatened by powerful neighbors. He brought order to the land and maintained his country's independence. Vlad was a harsh and cruel ruler, though. He had thousands of criminals and prisoners of war impaled on wooden stakes—a slow and painful death.

A map showing Transylvania, home of Count Dracula. Transylvania and neighboring Wallachia are in modern-day Romania.

VAMPIRE MANIA

People in Western Europe knew about vampires long before *Dracula* was published. In the early 18th century, vampire fever swept through Eastern Europe. Mass vampire sightings and corpse stakings became common. The first reports of these vampires from the east reached the European cities of the west and were an overnight sensation.

Varney the Vampire was published in the 1840s.

VAMPIRES AND THE PUBLIC

Soon, vampires began to appear in print. In 1819 John William Polidori wrote *The Vampyre*. Although vampires had previously featured in poetry, it was the first vampire novel to be published. *The Vampyre* was an instant success and other vampire books followed, including *Dracula*. In addition to novels, vampire plays and operas were produced.

A poster (top) for the 1927 stage production of Dracula. It starred Bela Lugosi, who went on to play the Count a number of times in films.
A still from Nosferatu (bottom), an early film based on the Dracula story.

MODERN VAMPIRES

Count Dracula would become even more well known through his appearances in the cinema. The first film to feature a vampire was *Vampire of the Coast*, in 1909. Since then hundreds have been made, proving just how popular they are. Vampires have also found their way onto television screens with series such as *Buffy the Vampire Slayer* and *Angel*. Today, rather than being evil villains, vampires are more likely to be romantic heroes in novels such as Anne Rice's *Vampire Chronicles* and Stephenie Meyer's four-book *Twilight* saga.

THE BEAST OF CROGLIN GRANGE

A VAMPIRE TALE FROM 17TH-CENTURY ENGLAND

ANNE CRANSWELL AND HER BROTHERS HAD ONLY RECENTLY MOVED INTO CROGLIN GRANGE, BUT THEY QUICKLY MADE THEMSELVES AT HOME.

WHILE ANNE LOOKED AFTER THE HOUSE, HER BROTHERS, EDWARD AND MICHAEL, RAN THE FARM.

THE DAY HAD BEEN HOT AND LONG. ANNE DECIDED TO GO TO BED EARLY THAT NIGHT.

SLEEP WELL, ANNE.

THANK YOU, EDWARD, I WILL.

OUT IN THE GARDEN WERE TWO TINY POINTS OF RED LIGHT. THE TWO BLAZING SPARKS BOBBED FROM SIDE TO SIDE, ALL THE TIME GETTING LARGER AND LARGER. WITH SHOCK, ANNE REALIZED SHE WAS STARING AT A PAIR OF FIERY EYES—AND THEY WERE STARING BACK AT HER.

SOON THE EYES WERE AT HER WINDOW. IT WAS TOO DARK FOR ANNE TO SEE CLEARLY WHO OR WHAT WAS THERE, BUT SHE COULD HEAR IT—SCRATCHING AND TAPPING SOUNDS FILLED THE ROOM.

GASP!

WHO'S THERE? WHAT DO YOU WANT?

SHARP FINGERNAILS WERE PICKING AT THE WINDOW LEAD, PEELING BACK THE SOFT METAL STRIPS THAT HELD THE PANES OF GLASS.

BONY FINGERS PUSHED, AND A PANE OF GLASS FELL.

A MISSHAPEN HAND REACHED THROUGH THE HOLE, GRASPED THE WINDOW LATCH, AND TURNED IT.

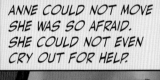

ANNE COULD NOT MOVE SHE WAS SO AFRAID. SHE COULD NOT EVEN CRY OUT FOR HELP.

THE WINDOW OPENED. NOW ANNE COULD CLEARLY SEE THE CREATURE.

THE DOOR IS LOCKED FROM THE INSIDE!

THE BROTHERS BURST INTO THE BEDROOM. OVER THE UNCONSCIOUS BODY OF THEIR SISTER CROUCHED A HIDEOUS MONSTER.

IT HAD BITTEN HER.

SZHAHHH!

BREAK IT OPEN!

BEFORE THE BROTHERS COULD MOVE, THE CREATURE WAS AT THE WINDOW AND HAD FLED INTO THE GARDEN.

THE BROTHERS PURSUED THE MONSTER TO THE BACK OF THE GARDEN, WHERE A HIGH WALL SEPARATED IT FROM THE CHURCHYARD NEXT DOOR.

THE BEAST SPRUNG INTO THE AIR...

...AND VANISHED.

ANNE CRANSWELL WAS SENT AWAY TO RECOVER. SHE RETURNED TO THE GRANGE THE FOLLOWING YEAR.

I AM GLAD TO BE BACK, EDWARD, BUT I AM STILL HAUNTED BY THE MEMORY OF THAT NIGHT.

YOU NEED NOT WORRY, ANNE. THERE HAVE BEEN NO FURTHER ATTACKS.

IN ALL LIKELIHOOD THE BEAST HAS LONG SINCE LEFT THE AREA.

TO SET YOUR MIND AT EASE...

...I HAVE INSTRUCTED THE FARM HANDS TO KEEP A CAREFUL WATCH FOR STRANGERS.

AND SHOULD THE CREATURE RETURN...

...IT WILL BE MET BY A VOLLEY OF PISTOL FIRE!

THE NEXT MORNING, THE BROTHERS AND TWO FARMHANDS WENT TO THE CHURCHYARD.

DO YOU THINK YOUR SHOT HIT THE CREATURE, EDWARD?

I CANNOT SAY FOR CERTAIN. IT ROSE INTO THE AIR AND VANISHED.

I SEE NO BLOOD.

THE DOOR TO THE CRYPT IS OPEN!

GET A LANTERN. IT MAY BE HIDING IN THERE.

THE MEN ENTERED THE CRYPT. INSIDE IT THE COFFINS HAD BEEN TOSSED AROUND.

WHO HAS DONE THIS?

THIS COFFIN IS UNTOUCHED.

18

THEY LIFTED THE COFFIN LID. INSIDE WAS A BODY, SHRIVELLED AND BROWN WITH AGE.

IT IS NOT ROTTEN BUT DRIED THROUGH!

THERE IS A FRESH WOUND ON ITS LEG.

HAND ME YOUR KNIFE.

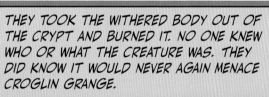

MICHAEL DUG INTO THE WOUND.

A PISTOL BALL! YOUR SHOT FOUND ITS MARK AFTER ALL, EDWARD.

IT IS THE THING YOU CHASED LAST NIGHT—ONE OF THE UNDEAD, A BLOOD DRINKER!

THEY TOOK THE WITHERED BODY OUT OF THE CRYPT AND BURNED IT. NO ONE KNEW WHO OR WHAT THE CREATURE WAS. THEY DID KNOW IT WOULD NEVER AGAIN MENACE CROGLIN GRANGE.

WE MUST DESTROY IT OR YOUR SISTER WILL NEVER BE FREE OF ITS CURSE.

THE END

OF THE 17 BODIES FLUCKINGER EXAMINED, 12 APPEARED TO BE FRESH.

I AM BAFFLED, CAPTAIN. THESE BODIES ARE NOT NORMAL.

THE VILLAGERS SAY IT IS THE WORK OF THE SUPERNATURAL. THEY CLAIM THE DEAD ARE RISING FROM THEIR GRAVES, HUNTING DOWN THE LIVING, AND DRINKING THEIR BLOOD. THEY HAVE A NAME FOR THESE UNDEAD BEINGS—VAMPIRES.

EXCUSE ME DOCTOR, THERE IS A VILLAGER OUTSIDE.

HE SAYS HE HAS INFORMATION ABOUT THE DEATHS.

WELL? WHAT IS IT YOU HAVE TO SAY?

YOUR HONOR, THIS ISN'T THE FIRST TIME OUR VILLAGE HAS SUFFERED SUCH STRANGE DEATHS.

FIVE YEARS AGO, A HAJDUK* CAME TO LIVE HERE. HIS NAME WAS ARNONT PAULE**.

*A SERBIAN MILITIAMAN.
**ALSO SPELLED ARNOLD PAOLE AND ARNOND PAVLE.

22

ARNONT PAULE HAD BEEN IN THE SOUTH, FIGHTING FOR THE AUSTRIAN ARMY.

AS PAYMENT FOR PAULE'S MILITARY SERVICE, THE AUSTRIANS GRANTED HIM A SMALL PARCEL OF FARMLAND. WHEN THE WAR ENDED, HE TRAVELED NORTH TO HIS NEW HOME IN THE VILLAGE OF MEDVEGYA.

PAULE WAS IN KOSOVO ON HIS WAY BACK TO SERBIA WHEN...

BY 1727, ARNONT PAULE WAS SETTLED IN MEDVEGYA, WORKING HIS SMALL FARM.

HIS PEACE DID NOT LAST LONG.

AHHH!

ARNONT PAULE WAS KILLED IN AN ACCIDENT.

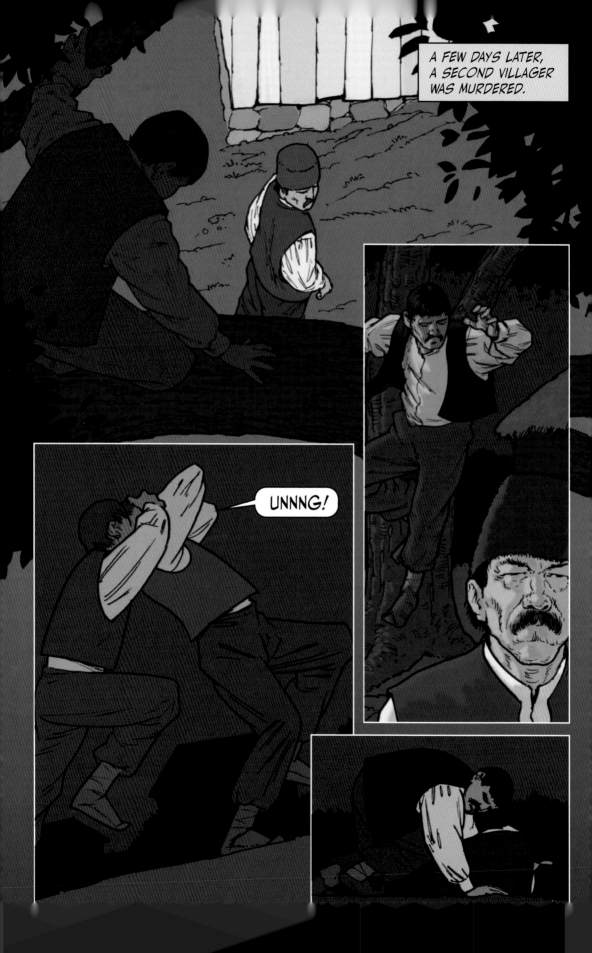

FEAR SPREAD THROUGH THE VILLAGE. ONLY THE BRAVE DARED TRAVEL ALONE AT NIGHT.

THEY DID NOT FEEL SAFE EVEN IN THEIR OWN HOMES.

THE VILLAGERS' PRECAUTIONS DID NOT STOP A THIRD MURDER.

NO ONE KNEW WHO THE ATTACKER WAS UNTIL...

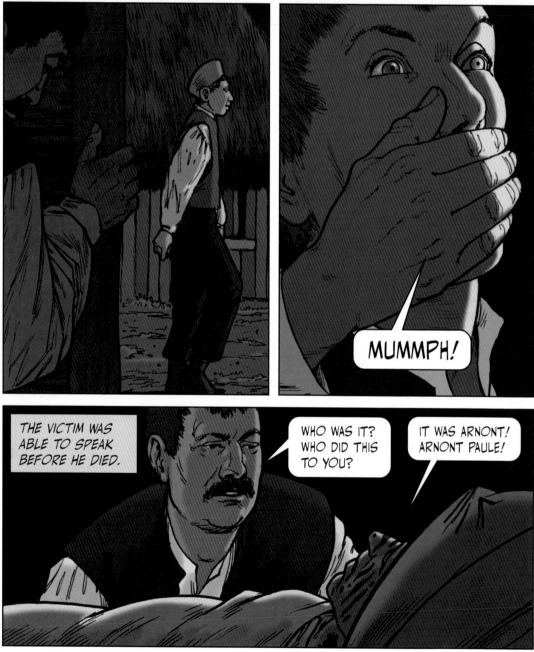

THE VILLAGERS HELD A MEETING TO DECIDE WHAT TO DO.

...BUT IT'S IMPOSSIBLE! I WAS THERE WHEN HE WAS BURIED—WE ALL WERE! HOW CAN A DEAD MAN BE THE MURDERER?

IT IS POSSIBLE. I HAVE SEEN IT IN THE SOUTH. DO YOU REMEMBER HOW ARNONT USED TO TELL US HOW HE HAD BEEN BITTEN BY A VAMPIRE AND HAD CURED HIMSELF?

WELL, IT SEEMS HIS CURE DID NOT WORK. ARNONT PAULE HAS BECOME ONE OF THE UNDEAD, A VAMPIRE.

AND BEFORE LONG PAULE'S VICTIMS WILL BECOME LIKE HIM. THEY WILL LEAVE THEIR GRAVES IN SEARCH OF BLOOD.

WHAT CAN WE DO? HOW CAN YOU KILL WHAT IS ALREADY DEAD? WILL WE HAVE TO ABANDON OUR HOMES?

NO, BUT WE MUST ACT NOW...

...OR THIS VILLAGE WILL BECOME ALIVE WITH VAMPIRES!

THE VILLAGERS MARCHED TO THE GRAVEYARD...

...AND DUG UP PAULE'S COFFIN.

THEY TOOK OFF THE COFFIN LID.

LOOK AT HIS FACE! IT'S PINK! AND THERE'S BLOOD EVERYWHERE—FROM HIS MOUTH, HIS EYES AND NOSE, AND EVEN HIS EARS!

SEE HIS HANDS? THE SKIN AND NAILS HAVE COME AWAY, AND THERE ARE NEW ONES GROWING UNDERNEATH.

IF HE IS A VAMPIRE, THIS WILL FINISH HIM.

SCHUNKK!

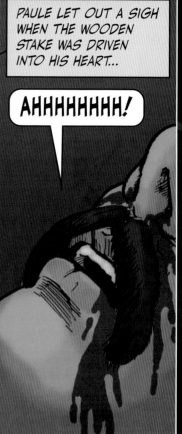

PAULE LET OUT A SIGH WHEN THE WOODEN STAKE WAS DRIVEN INTO HIS HEART...

AHHHHHHHH!

...AND HIS SHIRT BECAME SOAKED WITH BLOOD.

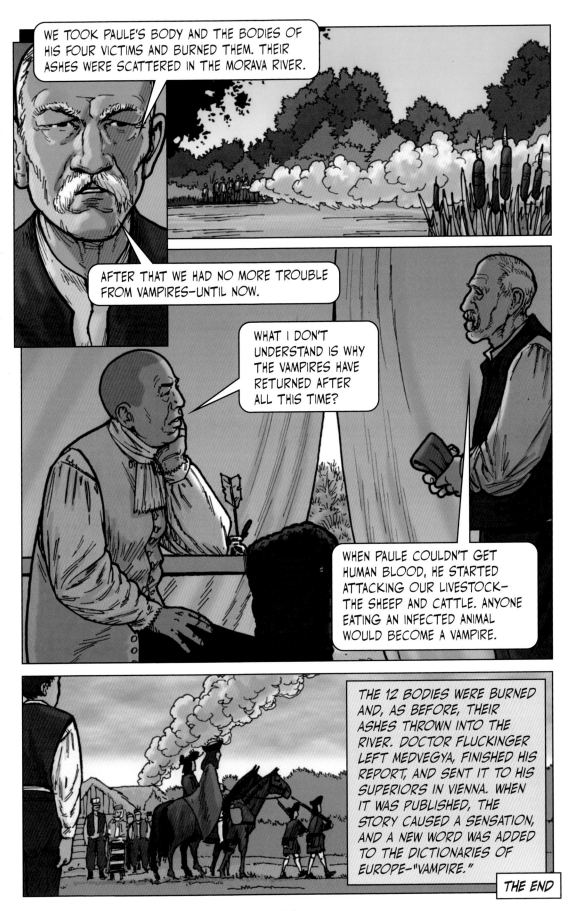

THE MERCY BROWN INCIDENT
THE RHODE ISLAND VAMPIRE, 1891

EDWIN BROWN WAS BACK HOME. HE HAD SPENT THE LAST YEAR IN COLORADO SPRINGS. HIS DOCTOR THOUGHT THE HEALTH RESORT'S WARM, DRY AIR WOULD CURE HIS DISEASED LUNGS.

IT DID NOT, SO, IN THE WINTER OF 1891, HE RETURNED TO EXETER, THE SMALL RHODE ISLAND FARMING COMMUNITY WHERE HE HAD GROWN UP.

EDWIN'S FATHER, GEORGE, WAS A WIDOWER WHO LIVED ON A SMALL FARM WITH HIS THREE DAUGHTERS.

ISN'T THAT DOCTOR METCALF'S BUGGY, PA?

HE'S HERE TO SEE LENA*. SHE HASN'T BEEN WELL THESE PAST FEW WEEKS.

GEORGE, WE NEED TO TALK.

*MOST PEOPLE CALLED MERCY BY HER MIDDLE NAME, "LENA."

EDDIE, GO INSIDE. SAY HELLO TO YOUR SISTERS.

CONSUMPTION—SO CALLED BECAUSE THE DISEASE SEEMED TO CONSUME THE SUFFERER. THE VICTIM'S BODY WASTED AWAY AS APPETITE FAILED AND LUNGS FILLED WITH BLOOD AND PUS. DOCTORS CALLED IT TUBERCULOSIS, AND IT WAS NEARLY ALWAYS FATAL. IT HAD KILLED GEORGE BROWN'S WIFE, MARY, AND HIS ELDEST DAUGHTER, MARY OLIVE. IT WAS SLOWLY KILLING HIS SON, AND HAD NOW INFECTED HIS SECOND DAUGHTER, LENA.

OVER THE NEXT MONTH, LENA BROWN'S CONDITION WORSENED, AND, ON JANUARY 17, SHE DIED. SHE WAS ONLY 19 YEARS OLD.

AFTER LENA'S DEATH, EDWIN'S ILLNESS BECAME MORE SEVERE. THE DISEASE BROUGHT ON FEVERS—AND NIGHTMARES.

LENA?

NEWS OF EDWIN'S DREAM SPREAD THROUGH THE SMALL COMMUNITY. ON MARCH 17, GEORGE BROWN'S NEIGHBORS PAID HIM A VISIT.

TOO MANY HAVE DIED OF THE SICKNESS THIS PAST WINTER, GEORGE. DOC METCALF CAN'T HELP US. WE HAVE TO HELP OURSELVES.

THE DISEASE IS BEING PASSED ON AFTER DEATH. GEORGE, WE'VE GOT TO SEE THE BODIES, MARY AND THE GIRLS. WE NEED TO KNOW IF THEY'VE BEEN SPREADING IT.

BUT IT'S MY FAMILY. CAN'T THEY BE LEFT IN PEACE?

COUGH! COUGH!

WE'RE JUST TRYING TO PROTECT OUR FAMILIES, GEORGE.

AND IT'S THE ONLY CHANCE YOU'VE GOT OF SAVING EDDIE HERE.

THE BAND OF MEN MARCHED TO CHESTNUT HILL CEMETERY. THE GRAVES OF GEORGE BROWN'S WIFE, MARY, AND HIS DAUGHTER, MARY OLIVE, WERE DUG UP...

GEORGE, YOU DON'T NEED TO BE A PART OF THIS IF YOU DON'T WANT TO.

I WANT TO STAY.

THE HEART WAS TAKEN OUTSIDE, BURNED...

...AND THE ASHES MIXED WITH WATER.

EDDIE, YOU HAVE TO DRINK IT. IT'LL HELP HEAL THE SICKNESS.

UGH!

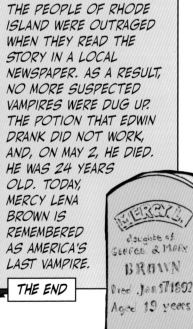

THE PEOPLE OF RHODE ISLAND WERE OUTRAGED WHEN THEY READ THE STORY IN A LOCAL NEWSPAPER. AS A RESULT, NO MORE SUSPECTED VAMPIRES WERE DUG UP. THE POTION THAT EDWIN DRANK DID NOT WORK, AND, ON MAY 2, HE DIED. HE WAS 24 YEARS OLD. TODAY, MERCY LENA BROWN IS REMEMBERED AS AMERICA'S LAST VAMPIRE.

THE END

MERCY L.
daughter of
GEORGE & MARY
BROWN
Died Jan 17 1892
Aged 19 years

MORE VAMPIRE STORIES

Here are three more
terrifying vampire tales to
thrill the heart and chill the blood.

THE VAMPIRE KING

There once lived in Ireland a chieftain and magician
called Abhartach. He was cruel and vicious and was
hated by his subjects. They longed to be rid of him but
were afraid of his magical powers.

They went to see Cathain, the chieftain of the neighboring land,
and pleaded with him to help them. He agreed and killed the
wicked king. Cathain buried Abhartach standing up, as was the
custom. However, Abhartach did not stay buried and, the
following day, was back. He demanded that his subjects cut their
wrists and fill bowls with their blood for him to drink. Cathain
returned and again defeated the evil chieftain. Again Abhartach
came back from the dead and ordered more bowls of blood.

This time Cathain went to see the Druids. They said that
Abhartach's magic powers had turned him into a *marbh bheo*, one
of the walking dead, but they knew how to kill the chieftain for
good. The next day Cathain faced the dead magician for a third
time. He slew the tyrant with a sword made from the wood of a
yew tree and buried him upside down. Around the grave, he
planted thorn trees. On top of the grave, Cathain placed a huge
stone. At last, Abhartach stayed in his tomb. Today, the site has an
evil reputation and few local people will go near it after dark.

THE SMILING VAMPIRE

When Jure Grando died, no one in Kringa, the Croatian town
where he had lived, thought they would ever see him again—
alive. They were wrong. It was 1672. Grando had died 16 years
earlier, yet people claimed to have seen him wandering through
the town at night. Every so often, he would stop at a house. A few
days later, someone in that house would die.

The townsfolk were terrified. The local priest went to see Grando's widow. She told him that her dead husband had been visiting her at night and drinking her blood. The priest was convinced that Grando was a vampire and, with a few brave men, went to Grando's grave.

They dug up the coffin and opened it. Grando's body was fresh, and a smile was on his lips. They took a wooden stake and tried to drive it into the vampire's heart, but it would not penetrate the chest. In desperation, one of the men picked up a spade and cut off Grando's head. For a time, the body jerked uncontrollably and blood flowed into the coffin. It worked, and Jure Grando did not trouble the people of Kringa again.

THE VAMPIRE OF KISILOVA

The last person Peter Plogojowitz's son expected to see that night was his father. A noise had woken him, and he had gone to investigate. There in the kitchen stood his father, demanding to be fed—but his father had been dead for over three days.

It was 1725. Sixty-two-year-old Peter Plogojowitz had been a farmer in the Serbian village of Kisilova. His death had been unexpected and was a loss to the village since he was well liked. He appeared a second time two days later, again asking for food. When his son refused, Plogojowitz left, giving him an evil stare. The next day, the son was dead.

His was the first of nine deaths in the village, all of them within a week. Before they died, each victim claimed to have had a dream. In it, Plogojowitz had entered their bedroom, grasped them by their throat, and had bitten them. The terrified villagers were panic-stricken and called on the authorities to help.

A detachment from the Austrian army arrived, and Plogojowitz's body was dug up. What they saw amazed them. The corpse was fresh and had not begun to decay. The hair had grown, while new fingernails and skin grew beneath the old. The face was red and plump, and dried blood was caked around the mouth. It was clear to the villagers—Plogojowitz was a vampire.

They acted swiftly. A wooden stake was driven through the vampire's heart. Large amounts of blood poured from the wound and from his mouth, nose, and ears. The body was then burned and the ashes thrown into the nearby river.

GLOSSARY

appetite The desire to eat.

autopsy The examination of a body to find out the cause of death.

baffled Puzzled.

bloated Swollen.

buggy A small, two-person, horse-drawn vehicle.

charm An object believed to have magic powers.

circumstances The facts surrounding an event.

corpse The body of a dead person.

crypt A room beneath a church used as a chapel or burial place.

engraving A design cut into a hard surface such as metal or wood.

garlic A strong tasting bulb of the lily family of plants.

Gothic A Victorian style of art and literature noted for its gloomy and horrific themes.

grange A country house with an attached farm.

haunts Places frequently used by specific types of people.

infected Diseased.

lair A hiding place.

livestock Farm animals kept for commercial reasons.

lore The collected knowledge and traditions of a subject.

militiaman A member of a military force made up of civilians.

operas Theatrical works for musicians and singers.

Persian Coming from ancient Persia (modern-day Iran).

precautions Steps taken to prevent an undesirable event from happening.

pus A thick yellow-green liquid made up of dead cells and bacteria, usually found in wounds.

rebelling Rising up in opposition to an established ruler.

resort A place people go to for a holiday or for their health.

shroud A sheet of cloth used to wrap a dead body.

torment To inflict physical or mental suffering on someone.

viscera The internal organs and intestines of the body.

widower A man whose wife has died.

withered Dried or shrunken.

FOR MORE INFORMATION

ORGANIZATIONS

How Stuff Works: Vampires
http://science.howstuffworks.com/science-vs-myth/strange-creatures/vampire.htm

The Vampire Library
http://www.vampirelibrary.com/

FURTHER READING

Barnhill, Kelly Regan. *Blood-Sucking, Man-Eating Monsters.* Mankato, MN: Capstone Press, 2009.

Besel, Jennifer M. *Vampires.* Mankato, MN: Capstone Press, 2006.

Brookes, Archer. *Vampireology: The True History of the Fallen.* Cambridge, MA: Candlewick Press, 2010.

Ganeri, Anita. *An Illustrated Guide to Mythical Creatures.* New York, NY: Hammond, 2009.

Ganeri, Anita. *Vampires and the Undead* (The Dark Side). New York, NY: PowerKids Press, 2010.

Gee, Joshua. *Encyclopedia Horrifica.* New York, NY: Scholastic, 2008.

Krensky, Stephen. *Vampires.* Brookfield, CT: Millbrook Press, 2006.

Rooney, Anne. *Vampire Castle.* New York, NY: Crabtree Publishing Company, 2008.

INDEX

Web Sites

Due to the changing nature of Internet links, Rosen Publishing has developed an online list of Web sites related to the subject of this book. This site is updated regularly. Please use this link to access the list:

http://www.rosenlinks.com/gts/vamp